In the Valley of Darkness

In the Valley of Darkness

ALDIVAN TORRES

Canary Of Joy

CONTENTS

1   In The Valley Of Darkness   1

1

In the Valley of Darkness

Aldivan Torres

In the Valley of Darkness

Author: Aldivan Torres
© 2020- Aldivan Torres
All rights reserved.

This book, including all its parts, is protected by Copyright and cannot be reproduced without author's permission, or transferred.

Aldivan Torres, born in Brazil, is a consolidated writer in various genres. So far, the titles have been published in dozens of languages. Since his age, he's always been a lover of the art of writing, having consolidated a professional career from the second semester of 2013. Your mission is to conquer the heart of each of your readers. In addition to literature, its main amusements are music, travels, friends, family, and the pleasure of life itself. "For literature, equality, fraternity, justice, dignity, and honor of human being always" is your motto.

In the Valley of Darkness
In the Valley of Darkness
Scene 1- In the living room
Scene 2- Church
Scene 3- In the living room
Scene 4- In the garden
Scene 5- Kitchen
Scene 6- Party
Scene 7- In Catherine's Living Room
Scene 8- on the road walking horse
Scene 9- At the fair
Scene 10- Appearance of St. Anthony and Mary at Site Guard
Scene 11- Assault
Scene 12- arrival of the cangaceiros
Scene 13- Clash
SCENE 14- At the lake
Scene 15- Engagement
At his girlfriend's house
Beginning of the disputes in the Paraguay War
Triple alliance treaty
The Nurse
In forest
In Forest 2
In Family
Talking to a fighter

Scene 1- In the living room

Mary
Are you ready, Anthony? It's almost time to go to church.
Anthony

I'm ready, mom. I'm glad to participate in the confirmation. It is a special moment of Christian confirmation.

Mary

I rejoice in that. Today is the day to reveal a secret. Your delivery was very difficult. It was hours of agony. Hopelessly, the midwife made a promise to Saint Anthony. If you survived, she would give you that name in honor of the saint's miracle. So it happened. You survived and were called Anthony.

Anthony

Amazing! Thank you so much for my life. Who is this saint, Anthony? Could you tell me a little of your story?

Mary

Of course, son. Born in Lisbon, he made his first Christian studies at the Sé Church of Lisbon. Years later, he requested a transfer to the Santa Cruz's Monastery of Coimbra, where he perfected his formation. On this occasion, he lived with the Franciscan missionaries, who were later killed for faith. It inspired him to seek his own way. Traveled to Morocco. But due to illness, he had to return without fulfilling his mission of evangelization. Later, he met Francis of Assisi and his followers, being this a milestone in their Christian formation. From then on, convinced of his vocation, he did a beautiful pastoral work. He always believed in Christian principles, a true way to the salvation of the soul. Therefore, he is the protector of all who require his intercession.

Anthony

As of today, I give myself entirely to your protection.

Mary

It's fine, son. He won't forsake you. Even though you are "In the valley of darkness," your salvation is certain.

Anthony

I'm confident in that, Mom. Are we go to church?

Mary

Let's go! It is the exact time.

Scene 2- Church

Priest

Brothers and sisters, we are gathered here to celebrate the Christian confirmation of these beloved young people in our community. Each one with his history has found in God a protection and refuge against the ills of life. It is this faith that moves them to Christ, the redeemer of all humanity. Therefore, I declare you, confirmed and anointed by the Christian faith.

Someone
Long live the Confirmed!
All
Alive!
Priest
Long live Christ!
All
Alive!
Priest
Go in peace and may the Lord accompany you!
All
Amen!

Scene 3- In the living room

Mary
How was this experience, Anthony?
Anthony
Excellent. I felt the presence of my protector all the time.
Mary
That's great. Always remember to be a good, hardworking and respectful boy. Always collaborate with people. This will bring you great reward.
Anthony
I always act like this. I have my flaws, but the qualities surpass. Furthermore, I'm grateful for being good.

Mary
And I thank you for be my son. Now, go to the field to help your father. We must harvest to put food on the table.

Anthony
I know, mom. I'm on my way.

Scene 4- In the garden

Anthony
I arrived, dad. I am ready to work!

Joseph
That's good, son! I really need your help. Go pick the corn, so we can make hominy, cake, and tamales. Today is the day to celebrate this significant day. The day of his consecration to Christ and to St. Anthony.

Anthony
Will be excellent! I need to have fun!

Joseph
I'm preparing you a surprise. Go and complete your task.

Anthony
What is a surprise?

Joseph
Please, no questions asked. Go to work!

Anthony
All right, dad!

Anthony
I have finished the job. Let's go home?

Joseph
Of course, son. Your mother must be worried, waiting for us.

Scene 5- Kitchen

Joseph
We're here, woman! We brought the necessary food to prepare the banquet.

Mary

Perfect, my man. I will start preparing delicious things for you and for the guests who will arrive.

Joseph

Excellent! Meanwhile, I will read a book!

Anthony

Thank you both for your efforts. I feel that I am important to each of you.

Joseph

For sure, my son. But there will come a day when you will take your destiny. You will have your family and will beget your children, my grandchildren.

Anthony

True, that day will come. But I'll always be around. I am grateful for what you have done for me until now.

Mary

We know that. That is why you deserve divine protection.

Antonio

"Though I am in the valley of darkness," I will be saved.

Scene 6- Party

Joseph

Welcome to my humble home. Long time no see, *Escobar family*!

Romero

Exactly eight years ago, dear friend. We came back to stay. Working in the south, we got money and bought good land around Frexeira. We hope to be happy here.

Joseph

Will surely be because they will be close to the friends.

Amanda

I'll miss the south because of the cold and of the amenities. However, where my husband is, I will be. I am a faithful woman and I honor my commitment made in marriage.

Mary
You are just like me, an honorable woman. That's why we never got divorced. Men know how to recognize our qualities. Welcome.
Amanda
Thanks, friend.
Anthony
This is Catherine, that little child who left here? How beautiful it is.
Catherine
Good of you, you are stronger and more beautiful. The sun seems to have done you some good.
Anthony
How cute! We were the best friends in childhood. We climbed the trees to suck fruit, bathed in the river, invented a thousand jokes to distract ourselves, walked hand in hand, did homework together, we were so friends that people said we were boyfriends.
Catherine
I remember all that. I miss that blessed childhood. Now that I'm back, I always want to keep in touch. When you want to show up at home, you are welcome.
Anthony
Thank you for your kindness. The reciprocal is also true.
Catherine
Congratulations on your confirmation. Follows in your devotion that you will conquer everything in life. The man of faith is not shaken by the obstacles of life. Be a house built on rock and the storm will not get you down.
Anthony
I'm sure of it. The secret of success is work, persistence, and faith. I will remember your advice. It will guide me on the roads of life.
Catherine
Go put a song on for me. I want to dance.
Anthony
Me too! Let's have fun. Today is a day of celebration!

Scene 7- In Catherine's Living Room

Anthony

Good morning, darling. I'm going to town to buy some groceries for my dad. Want to join me?

Catherine

Will you let me go, mom?

Amanda

Of course, daughter. Anthony is an honorable young man. He will respect her. Furthermore, we need to buy supplies too.

Anthony

Great. So, let's go!

Catherine

I'm going!

Scene 8- on the road walking horse

Anthony

Tell me, Catherine, how was your passage in the south. It was eight years of separation between us.

Catherine

It was a long learning period. I studied at a college of nuns and got in touch with original Christianity. It made me reflect on the most varied contexts of life. I learned that we are free, and we have the right to be happy no matter what we are. Against this, we suffer from the prejudice of the family. We are slaves of men. We are said inferior by moral customs. However, Christ never preached this. And you? How did you spend these eight years?

Anthony

I passed with the grace of God. Here in the northeast, life is very difficult. We face drought, criminals, outlaws, and lack of government investment among other things. But that never discouraged me. I am a strong and brave man. I believe northeast Brazil still has a good future. Regarding your reflection, I agree with you. We are equal before God and this is how I will treat my wife when I get married.

Catherine

Congratulations! You are a man ahead of your time. A little more and I'm falling in love. Joking aside, any woman would be honored to be his wife.

Anthony

Any man would also be honored to be her husband. But, as the saying goes, one thing at a time. We will still have many moments of conviviality. That way we will get to know each other better.

Catherine

You are completely right. We are very young and inexperienced. I really believe in fate. Whatever will be, will be.

Anthony

Exact. We are already close to our goal.

Scene 9- At the fair

Anthony

We have here the largest fair in the interior of the state. I'm glad we have plenty of options.

Catherine

Excellent! I'm curious. Could you explain the importance of Cimbres in the current context?

Anthony

It is one of the most important points of the state. It retains colonial architecture, historical monuments and even a chamber senate that is the main center of political decision. Furthermore, it is a place with influence throughout the state.

Catherine

Perfect to have this foothold. I will take plenty of fruits and food. We need to fuel the pantry.

Anthony

I will also buy provisions for the whole month. On the way back, we'll pass the guard's place. Something drives me on this path.

Catherine

It must be something related to your protector. The guard's place is a mysterious place. I want to go there too.

Anthony

Let's go then! We already bought everything we need.

Scene 10- Appearance of St. Anthony and Mary at Site Guard

Catherine and Anthony rest. At this moment, a man, and a woman introduce themselves to them.

Anthony

Who are you?

Mary

I am the grace, protector of this place.

Saint Anthony

I am Anthony, your holy protector.

Catherine

What do you wish?

Mary

Bless you and give you a warning. If the world does not submit to my beloved Christ, it will conflict.

Anthony

What can we do?

Saint Anthony

Pray the Holy Rosary fervently. Together with my mother, I will pray for you. As for you, my protégé, nothing will happen to you. I will be with you at all times.

Anthony

Thank you, my big brother.

Catherine

Will I marry Anthony, dear grace?

Mary

If you will, you will have my blessing. I will be your solace in the difficult times that are to come.

Catherine

Thank you! What about the outlaws? How can we protect ourselves?
Mary
Put bitter melon in your homes. I will send a protector spirit. These bad guys will not hurt you.
Catherine
Thankful! Be blessed forever.
Anthony
Many thanks to both of you. Glad to meet you at this sacred place.
Mary
I am the mother of humanity. I am everywhere. Always pray with me. We need to overcome evil.
Anthony
We will win, ma'am. If it depends on my faith, the victory is certain.
Saint Anthony
Be at peace and may God accompany you. We have to go now.

Scene 11- Assault

Antonio and Catarina are stopped on the road.
Burglar
Both of you! It's an assault!
Catherine
You can take everything I have. Don't hurt us.
Anthony
Stay calm. It can take everything!
Burglar
Good thing you guys are quiet. I promise not to hurt them. But I can't say the same thing about your village. The outlaws are on their way!
Catherine
My God! The outlaws. They will destroy us.
Anthony
Do not worry, Miss! God will protect us.
Catherine
I cannot be calm. They are terrible.

Burglar

The girl is right. We are ready to barbarize. No one will stop us.

Anthony

We'll tell the outlaws we're waiting. They may even win, but it will not be easy.

Burglar

I'll give the message. See you later, fools!

Scene 12- arrival of the cangaceiros

men

The outlaws are coming. Every man for himself!

Antonio

Be prepared. Put bitter melon covering the houses. The virgin will protect them.

Catherine

And you? What are you doing?

Antonio

I will join the others to defend the village. Do not worry about me. The good will protect me.

Mary

Go in peace, my son. Trust in saint Anthony.

Joseph

I'm going too. I won't leave you alone in this occasion.

Romero

You can count on me too. Let's beat these bad guys.

Catherine

Be cautious. I want everyone alive.

Antonio

Do not worry. We would be fine.

Scene 13- Clash

So, you are the men who will try to stop us from invading the village? You look pathetic.

Antonio

You are terrible, but God is with us. Furthermore, you will not do any harm!

War scenes

SCENE 14- At the lake

Catherine

I'm glad things worked out so well. I have afraid of those bad guys. I'm glad that God protected us.

Amanda

I was also terrified. We were saved by brave warriors and the most holy mother. May they never come back.

Romero

Will not return. They felt our strength, courage, and bravery.

Joseph

Unity is strength. The good will always overcome evil.

Antonio

I would not allow anyone to hurt you, my beloved. I love you.

Amanda

You're dating?

Catherine

Yes, mom. We want to get married and have our children. We'll be happy forever.

Amanda

I bless you.

Mary

You have all my support. I am pleased.

Romero

A good person. Cheers, my daughter.

Catherine

Thanks, Dad.

Joseph

The world meets nobody halfway. A childhood love that has been separated and is now reborn. That's why I believe in fate.

Antonio

If there is destiny, I don't know. I just know I'm pleased. What worries me now is this war between Brazil and Paraguay.

Catherine

What caused this war, love?

Antonio

The rivalry between the countries involved, motivated by cross-border disagreement, freedom of navigation and power struggle.

Catherine

I got it. Who ends up paying the price is the innocent? We live in a cruel world.

Amanda

That's too cruel, daughter. Where will we stop? I am very much afraid for our future.

Mary

The world needs prayer. May this war end soon for the good of every nation.

Joseph

So be it, woman. I believe the war was necessary because of the misunderstanding that was generated. We hope a good end to this.

Romero

Hopefully, compadre. Sometimes I'm not so optimistic. I believe this will bring major sequels to the parties involved. After all, there is no winner in a war.

Antonio

That's a big truth. We will all suffer. Whatever happens, my saint will be with me.

Mary

He won't abandon you. Even though you are "In the valley of darkness," your salvation is certain.

Antonio
I'm a firm believer in that myself.

Scene 15- Engagement

Mailman
I came to deliver a letter to Mr. Anthony Marinho.
Anthony
I'm here! Thank you so much for your attention!
Mailman
You're welcome! I just do my job!
Anthony
I am not believing! I was summoned to war. What will I do now?
Mary
My God! It's the worst news I've ever had. My son summoned to war. What will become of us and your girlfriend?
Anthony
I don't know, mom. Faith is the only thing left to us immediately.
Joseph
It is a really desperate situation. We are with you, son. You will get out of this.
Anthony
I'm confident, my father. My saint Anthony will be with me wherever I am. Now I have to go say goodbye to my girlfriend. I don't know what she will decide.
Joseph
Go in peace, Son. I will pray that she understands.
Mary
My prayers are with you. The virgin will enlighten you to make the best decision.
Anthony
So be it, my mother.
In The way
Anthony

Am I alone on this road? Alone and worried. What will happen in this war?

Saint Anthony

You're not alone, let me keep you company.

Anthony

Of course, my protector. What about my call to war?

Saint Anthony

It was written in its destiny. There is nothing to worry about. If you trust me, I will deliver you from all perils.

Anthony

I trust! I am happy with your protection. Let's go?

Saint Anthony

Yes, I will accompany you to your girlfriend's house.

Anthony

You know, my Saint Anthony, I was thinking about life and its challenges. Born in northeastern Brazil, I learned early to overcome challenges. This is a region forgotten by the authorities and the world. It is a suffered region.

Saint Anthony

But just like me, the countryman is a warrior. Despite all the negative retrospectives, we still believe in ourselves. The countryman is a fort. I believe I will get out of this uncomfortable situation.

Anthony

You told the truth. It is a region forgotten by the world but not by God. You are a precious man to God. Admired for his determination, strength, and courage.

Saint Anthony

Even though you are "In the valley of darkness," your salvation is certain. Good men will always be victorious. I am with you in this adventure. Do you have faith?

Anthony

With all my mind, soul and heart. If I didn't believe in God and you, I would have died. Every obstacle I faced and overcame, I owe you. Immediately, what strikes me is the certainty of your protection. You are my partner and my best friend. With you, I am a house built on rock where the storm cannot bring it down. The victory is already mine.

Saint Anthony

The victory is ours! I do not promise you a bed of roses in this new challenge. After all, it is a war. You will face hard times, loss of faith and much suffering. This war in Paraguay will go down in history and totally change your view of the world.

Anthony

I can't imagine the dimension that is a war. I am ready to fight and learn. I will honor my Brazilian title and do my best. At this time, the future is uncertain. But I will let faith guide me.

Saint Anthony

Very well. You are in the right way. Pray incessantly for the end of the war. Together, we will get the victory.

Anthony

I hope so, my angel.

Saint Anthony

Continue the walk. I will be your spiritual guard. Count on me.

Anthony

Thanks.

At his girlfriend's house

Anthony

I came to say goodbye, Catherine. I have just been summoned to war.

Catherine

Why did this have to happen? What will happen now?

Anthony

I have no idea. I just wanted to say that I love you.

Catherine

Love you too. I have faith that you will get out of this. We're getting married and having our children.

Anthony

Excellent your faith. But if the worst happens? I don't want you to keep waiting by a promise. You can get someone else. I will not be upset.

Catherine

Do not even think about it. My commitment is for one man only. Your protector will bring you back to me. I will wait as long as necessary.

Anthony

I am very touched by your words. When I'm away, remember our music.

Catherine

Sing her to me then!

Anthony starts singing the couple's song. In this style, you hug and kiss. It was the farewell before the war.

Catherine

How beautiful! I'll keep this song in mind. Go in peace and God bless us!

Anthony

Amen! I will remember you every day. May fate be fulfilled.

Beginning of the disputes in the Paraguay War

Jean

We are the force of Paraguay. Give yourself up, or you will have death!

Anthony

You are in greater number. We have no alternative but surrender.

Jean

Well thought. Good thing you guys have good sense.

Anthony

However, don't be happy. Soon other allied forces will come, and you will be in trouble.

Jean

We're ready for the fight.

Triple alliance treaty

Emperor

Gentlemen, after the provocation has been launched, after the insult perpetrated on our flag by the tyrant of Paraguay who governs you can tell you nothing but that the proclamations and the demonstrations will be translated into facts, and that in twenty-four hours we will be in barracks, Within a fortnight on the battlefield and in three months in Asunción. The following terms of the triple alliance treaty are defined: His Majesty the Emperor of Brazil, the Argentine Republic and the Eastern Republic of Uruguay unite in an offensive and defensive alliance in the war promoted by the Paraguayan Government. Not being the war against the people of Paraguay, but against their government. The Allies will be able to admit in a Paraguayan Legion the citizens of that nationality who want to compete to overthrow the said Government, and will give them the necessary elements, in the form and with the conditions that fit. Allies will compete with every means of war they may have, on land or in rivers, as they see fit.

War

Anthony

We arrived to defend the people of this city. Out, Paraguayans!

Jean

This is what we will see!

War Scenes

Captain

How did you feel in the first battle, recruit?

Anthony

It was a weird thing. Seeing all those people dying made me afraid and distressed.

Captain

Normal. This is just the beginning. This battle must last for a long time. Let's hope we're alive to tell the story.

Anthony

I have confidence in survival. I am young and have many dreams to fulfill. I want to have my children and rediscover my wife.

Captain

I'm rooting for your good. You can count on me. When we were struggling, I was intrigued. How didst thou 'escape?

Anthony

I have a supernatural strength by my side. My holy protector. Even though "I am in the Valley of Darkness", my salvation is certain.

Captain

Then it is explained. Your faith saves you. I'm not so lucky as you. I am a general without scruples and without love. God would never protect me.

Anthony

God loves everyone. Thank you for your help in battle. So, I will make a pact with you: Keep helping me and in return, I will ask for your life.

Captain

You are very generous. I don't know how to thank you. God bless you.

Anthony

You're welcome! Unity is strength.

Narration

The Battle of Riachuelo It was a strategic battle. At stake was the control of the silver basin that was the main mode of transportation of the time. The country that controlled the rivers would have great advantage over its opponent. The victory was Brazilian. Paraguayan forces have begun the siege of Uruguaiana but without operating options.

General Brazilian

Our opponents have no chance of winning. How about giving them a chance to surrender and prevent bloodshed?

Anthony

Good idea, General. We have to have humanity at these times.

General Brazilian

Truth. The Allies did not make war against Paraguay, but the tyrant Lopez, who rules them and treats them as slaves. Our purpose is to give them freedom and institutions by giving them a government of their own choosing.

General Paraguayan

As a military man, as a Paraguayan, and as a soldier defending the cause of institutions and the independence of his homeland, I reject your offer.

Soldier

Division officers and soldiers share the same opinion, and are all willing to succumb before accepting a proposal that dishonors and fills for the eternal Paraguayan soldier in infamy.

General Brazilian

Your forces are running out. Are you sure you want to avoid surrendering?

General Paraguayan

We will surrender with the following conditions: May our officers return to Paraguay or wherever they wish. May our soldiers not be delivered to the slaughter. May they be free.

General Brazilian

We accept your conditions. This battle is over.

The Nurse

Anthony

How are your patients, Ana?

Ana

Some better and some worse. I swear I'm working hard to cure them.

Anthony

I know it. You are an example. I got curious. Could you tell a little of your story?

Ana

Of course, yes. I was born in the interior of Bahia in a humble family but blessed by God. I married new and had three children. Two of them pursued a career in medicine and one in the military field. When they were summoned to this war, I felt obliged to accompany them. Here I am taking care of the sick and praying for the welfare of all. Now it's your turn. Tell me a little of your story.

Anthony

It's ok. I come from the interior of Pernambuco. I had to leave my fiancée and my parents for this war. My dream is to go home, have my offspring and forget about this war. She is so sad.

Ana

You're right. I am also sorrowful about this war. But I understand that it is an act of patriotism. We need to join forces against our enemy.

Anthony

Truth. Our love of the motherland being our top priority.

Ana

Now I got curious. You never got hurt in battle. What is the secret?

Anthony

I have a great protector. He accompanies me at all times. Even though I am "In the Valley of Darkness", my salvation is certain.

Ana

This is quite mystical. I also have my beliefs and values. That's why I'm here.

Anthony

Congratulations! I expect you to help more people. You are a national heroine.

Ana

Heroes are all who have lost their lives for this cause. Our freedom at the cost of the blood of many. This is the reality of this war.

Anthony

I hope to tell this story to my children and grandchildren.

Ana

Your faith saves you. I hope to find my family alive after this war.

Anthony

I wish the best for all combatants. You'll realize your dream.

Ana

Thank you!

In forest

General Brazilian

We need to do something. The money is gone and the spending on the troops only grows. Any suggestion?

Soldier

Let's ask England for money. It is our only way out.

General Brazilian

Well thought. We will pay this debt gradually. The defense of the motherland cannot wait.

Soldier

Exactly, sovereign.

In Forest 2

Captain

New supplies have just arrived. It appears that our Emperor is truly committed to this cause.

Anthony

It's the least he could do. We need to strengthen us to defeat the enemy.

Captain

Exactly. How do you feel?

Anthony

I miss my girlfriend and my family. I have no news of them, nor have they heard from me. This is tragic.

Captain

I understand. I'm very calm at this time. Focus on the current mission. Everything is right on time.

Anthony

I know, but the distance becomes painful. Being at war is a whole new situation for me. To survive, I have to kill and deceive. This is beyond my principles.

Captain

Learn once and for all: Only the strong survive the war. Forget all your moral values and survive. Think about your family and your girlfriend. We have a life out there.

Anthony

Thinking this way, the reason is with you. I promise to survive.

Captain

That's the spirit. Let's sleep now. The next few days promise.

In Family

Anthony

He was hit by an opponent! He is dead. I knew this boy. He had so many dreams. The war is over! It is unfortunate!

Captain

My God, what a pity! Rest in peace! May you receive the glory of the motherland.

Anthony

Not all glories can comfort the family! Damn war!

Mother

My God, he was my son! I'm torn! What will become of me? It was my dearest son.

Anthony

We are sorry! How do you feel now?

Mother

It is the worst pain a human being can have. He was an educated, hard-working and responsible boy. It helped everyone in the family. We spent many important moments together. He was cheerful, understanding, and loving to me. It was truly an angel from heaven.

Captain

My condolences. I'm speechless!

Mother

Thank you!

Anthony

We will make a good funeral. He deserves for his good service to a homeland. We will arrange immediately.

Mother

Thank you very much for your participation. It comforts me a lot!

Captain

Here we deliver this soldier's body. All honors and glory for those who defended the homeland with their life.

Anthony

Yes, we are witnesses of that. May the holy angels make him feel very welcome.

Mother

Thank you for the gift of being your mother. Thank you for every shared, moment next to you. He was with me in health, sickness, joy, and sadness. These were intense and unmissable moments.

Anthony

His grit and strength to win inspires me to continue my mission in war. I will not give up! I will continue caring for the sick for the love of the motherland. From now on, all soldiers will be my children. I will fight for each of them!

Mother

What an example! How many more will succumb? Man of God, why don't you ask your saint to end the war?

Anthony

I don't have such boldness. We need to understand that the war took place by free will of man and that is how it must end.

Mother

I understood. Forgive my intrusion.

Anthony

No problems.

Mother

I will ask for strength at this moment that my soul is torn. Pray for me, man of God.

Anthony

Of course, yes. It's going to be okay. For our beloved Brazilian homeland!

Captain

For our soldiers!

Mother

For our families!

Talking to a fighter

Anthony

How are you, master? Congratulations on your performance in the war.

Black man

Thanks. You too. For my good performance, I was granted freedom. It feels totally new to me. Finally, I can be considered a real person.

Anthony

How does it feel to be a slave? What did you suffer?

Black man

Were decades of humiliation and suffering in the coffee plantations. We were treated like animals by our owners. It was so painful.

Anthony

I guess. Justice has been done. To God, you have always been a human. We are all equal before him.

Black man

I was aware of that. But they denied my rights all the time. The law of man is perverse.

Anthony

You're right. Good thing this is over. You are now a free man.

Black man

But slavery is not over yet. I just received an award for my bravery in war. I feel sorry for my African brothers. They need to be free because that is their right.

Anthony

For sure. You will make it. God will help us. Once the war is over, continue your fight. I believe that the freedom of all slaves does not take long.

Black man

I hope so. And you? What did you leave behind with this war?

Anthony

I left my parents and my girlfriend in the northeast of Brazil. They must be worried about me. I have no way to give news.

Black man

That is sad! But I see there is a protection on your side. Continue in faith that your victories will be achieved.

Anthony

I will always trust God and my protector! Each deliverance is a victory! I have no doubt that I will be happy! I will still have my children and grandchildren. Furthermore, I will survive!

Black man

We are with you. Here there are many with this same dream. Not everyone can do it. Thousands have already lost their lives in this damn war. This is sorrowful.

Anthony

I'm used to it. In war is "Each for himself and God for all." There is no other way to survive.

Black man

I agree. May this war end soon!

Anthony

I wish the same.

Talking with Woman

Anthony

Hey, you're a woman! How do you fight in war?

Vanessa

You have discovered my secret! Do not tell anyone!

Anthony

It's ok! I will not tell! What's your name?

Vanessa

Vanessa. And you? What is your name?

Anthony

Anthony. Tell me, Miss, why did you risk so much coming for such a dangerous war?

Vanessa

My dream has always been to work in the military, but they never allowed me. I thought war was a perfect time to show my worth. So, I dress like a man to fool everyone in battle. So far, I have not lost any dispute. I have killed hundreds of men in honor of my homeland.

Anthony

A laudable goal. You are really incredible.

Vanessa

I see that you are also a beast in battle. Where did you come from, and what do you want when the war is over?

Anthony

I am from the countryside of Pernambuco. The son of farmers, I was about to get married when I was summoned to war. I hope to survive, return to my northeast and fulfill my dreams.

Vanessa

I hope you achieve. This is the bad side of war. Destroys unfinished lives and dreams.

Anthony

I remain hopeful through my faith. I am devoted to Saint Anthony who always protects me. Even though I'm in the Valley of Darkness, my salvation is certain.

Vanessa

Amazing. I also have my faith. I am devoted to Our Lady Aparecida.

Anthony

The patron saint of Brazil. Mother of all humanity. You could not be in better hands. Through faith we have divine protection and can perform miracles. We will win!

Vanessa

We have already won! Paraguay is broken due to our onslaughts. It will not be long before they abandon the war. You can believe what I'm saying.

Anthony

I believe! It raises my hopes and dreams. I can't wait to be at my place.

Vanessa

May God hear you! I'm leaving! Remember to keep my secret.

Anthony

Your secret is in good hands. Go in peace!

Vanessa

Thank you!

Talking

Xukuru Indian

I think I know you.

Anthony

Truth? Where?

Xukuru Indian

I saw you in Cimbres. I am the only Xukuru Indian who survived this war.

Anthony

How nice! These are the general of our troop and our nurse.

Nurse

Feel free!

General

Great Indian! I've seen you in battle!

Xukuru Indian

Thank you all.

Anthony

What happened to your friends?

Xukuru Indian

They failed in faith. One by one they were defeated by their enemies. There were sad and painful days.

Anthony

I understand. I have also lost several fight mates.

General

Those who lose strengthen the victors. Each will have their memory preserved as the nation's hero. No one wants to die, but this is the worthiest means: to die for your country.

Xukuru Indian

I agree. They are true heroes.

Nurse

I remember you. Furthermore, I've already treated your arm injury. Are you better?

Xukuru Indian

I'm great. Thank you for your care.

Nurse

You're welcome! I lost family members in the war. It was so tragic.

General

I lost a cousin. He was my faithful friend. Until now, I cry for him.

Xukuru Indian

My condolences!

General

I say the same!

General

See what war is: As she separates us from our family and promotes encounters. I strongly believe in fate, this force that can change our trajectory. Nothing happens by chance. Good spirits unite us and teach us. Pain also causes love. Wars also promote peace of mind and resolve conflicts. There is always a positive side to all misfortunes.

Anthony

Great sage! May the good be in our hearts!

General

He is always in each of our actions. That's why we survived. You granted me life through your protector and, in return, I support you. Life is a tangle of alliances. Only the strong survive!

Xukuru Indian

The strong become weak in pain. Difficulties give us strength in mission. Every life I save ennobles me. This leads me to important reflections. It is a learning that I will take for a lifetime.

Nurse

War destroys concepts and creates other unexpected situations. This is what I call conceptual adaptation. It is through this that we define the future.

General

Surely, our beloved homeland is in good hands and no matter what happens, we are already winners.

Xukuru Indian

Truth. Thanks for this chance. My spirit is at peace.

Anthony

The war is over! We won the last battle! We are saved!

Nurse

Didn't I say we would survive? The Victory is Brazilian!

General

Now that it's all over, what do you mean?

Anthony

I fulfilled what I promised. Are you alive? This proves that faith is the greatest force in the universe!

Nurse

You're right. Your faith makes you famous all over the country. Wherever you go, they are talking about you.

Anthony

I leave the glory to God. I am only a servant. When do we leave?

General

Today! Nice to meet you!

Anthony

The pleasure was all mine! May God bless you on your journey!

General

May God bless us all! Bye!

Anthony

I'm coming home with the mission accomplished. There were so many emotions and sadness lived. I feel totally transformed by the experience of war.

General

You grew up, young man. Now is to continue on with your dreams.

Anthony

Truth. Thank you for all your support. If it wasn't for your help, I wouldn't be here.

General

No need to thank. You deserve it because you are a good man. God bless you!

Anthony

So be it!

At home

Catherine

My God! Are you alive! I am not believing!

Anthony

I survived because of my faith. How are you? Already married?

Catherine

I was waiting for you. I belong to you.

Anthony

My love is yours. I want to avoid waiting any longer. Let's get married and have our children!

Catherine

It's all I ever wanted! Love won!

Anthony

Love Wins everything! Let's be happy forever!

The End

www.ingramcontent.com/pod-product-compliance
Lightning Source LLC
LaVergne TN
LVHW020448080526
838202LV00055B/5388